High School Reunion

Forced, Taboo, Dominant, Rough Swingers, Filthy Age Gap, Erotic Bedtime Short Sex Stories

Lana Kendra

This is a work of fiction; names, characters, places, and incidents are either the product of the author's imagination or are used fictitiously, and any resemblance to actual people, living or dead, business establishments, events, or locales is entirely coincidental.

This e-book is for your personal use only and may not be resold or given to anyone else. If you want to give this book to someone else, please buy an extra copy for each person. If you're reading this book and didn't buy it, or if it wasn't bought for your personal use only, go back to your favorite ebook retailer and buy your copy. Thank you for acknowledging this author's efforts.

Table of Contents

Content Warning

Due to its sexual content, this book is only for those over the age of legal adulthood. There are some topics with a lot of foul language. All of the characters are at least eighteen years old.

Introduction

Are you in search of an exciting and thrilling book to read? Look no further than this extensive collection of Erotic Suspense book. I offer a wide range of genres, including Romantic Erotica, Fantasy, and Urban BDSM Fiction, to cater to even the most discerning reader. Whether you enjoy Anthologies, Westerns, or Paranormal Romance, I have something to suit your taste. My collection also includes Poetic Folklore, Interracial, Black & African American Literary Criticism, and Gothic Horror for those who crave a deeper and darker reading experience. If you're interested in Futuristic, LGBTQ+, Short Stories, or Lesbian literature, my diverse range of options will keep you captivated. Additionally, I offer Humorous, Victorian, New Adult, and College Women's Psychological Mysteries for those seeking a lighter but equally engaging read. Furthermore, My Fairy Tale Collections,

Transgender, Contemporary Western, Bisexual, and Poetry genres will transport you to different worlds and explore a variety of themes. For my Teen and Young Adult readers, I have a selection of European Geography, Cultures, eBooks, Loners, Outcasts, Mythology, Folk Tales, and much more. With such a wide array of options to choose from, you'll never run out of thrilling and enchanting stories to immerse yourself in.

It is important to emphasize that this content is exclusively intended for individuals who are 18 years of age or older.

High School Reunion

Amidst her classmates gathered for their high school reunion, Rivka stood near the gymnasium door, feeling a little uncomfortable amid the sounds of laughter and clinking drinks. Years had passed since her last visit to this building, and a lot had happened. She had been an awkward and shy adolescent back then, frequently made fun of by her peers for defying their social expectations.

Throughout her all-girl high school years, she had been buried in a book, choosing them above the turmoil her friends seemed to be involved in all the time. After searching for a while, she eventually located a table with a few open seats. She took a seat next to Minky Korf, a silly woman who seemed to have not changed much in the past fifteen years, and she began to tell stories of adventures and antics to the other women in the group. Rivka chuckled too, relieved to have located a table close to the nice girls instead of some of her more poisonous classmates who had caused her so much grief.

The voice snapped Rivka out of her reverie, "Can I sit here?" Rivka realized she had thought too quickly as she looked up. Beside her, Sarah Andasi, who was arguably one of the most toxic females in her class, had her hand gripped on the seatback of the chair.

"I suppose so," Rivka replied, "but nobody's seated here yet."

Sarah's golden hair flowed in loose waves over her shoulders, giving her a boisterous, brazen appearance reminiscent of her high school days.

However, she also had a new quality to her that had not been there before: a hardness in her gaze. Perhaps it was the fact that she was facing Rivka, their anger towards each other evident even after all these years. Perhaps it was the recent divorce that had left her single and unable to figure out how to date as a middle-aged woman who no longer knew what she wanted. Whatever it was, Rivka felt uncomfortable.

Apparently sensing that Rivka was uncomfortable, Sarah introduced herself to Minky and the others right away, sharing personal anecdotes from their common background.

Rivka observed the group from a distance, observing the interactions between the former classmates without offering any commentary. While some performed unexpectedly well, others who appeared to be on the fast track to success when they were in school were stuck in dead-end professions.

"What about you, Rivka?" she asked, realizing she was the focus of the discussion. "How many locations does your fancy shmancy boutique have now?"

Rivka chuckled, enjoying Minky's consistency in making

sure everyone was part of the discourse. Her boutique clothing business had taken off after she hired a famous Orthodox Jewish influencer who brought in big clients. "We have five, with a sixth and seventh opening up in a few months," she said. Her little business, which had started off selling vintage-style clothes she had designed, grew into an empire, making her millions of dollars.

"Whoa, you really made it big haven't you?" Minky said with an astonished nod. That's incredible.

The statement "It could be worse, I could be making a living selling used junk" caught Rivka off guard as Sarah was obviously making a swipe at her while speaking to someone else.

"For a nice price, in a classy boutique." Rivka responded. "You should come by and try us out, I think there are three stores within five miles of your house"

"I don't remember asking you for your opinion, and it's

interesting that when I mentioned used junk you knew I was talking about your store" Sarah replied.

Minky remarked, "Knock it off, guys. We don't have to reenact everything from high school."

With a teasing glance at Rivka, Sarah shot back, her eyes flaming, "Why, are you hoping little Mrs. Millionaire will have you be the next influencer to make her store look more than it is?"

As Rivka cataloged all the things she wished she could say back, but knew better than to speak out loud, she felt heat rising in her cheeks. Sarah has always had a knack for getting under people's skin, especially Rivka. Now that she was happy with her life's direction, she knew better than to sink to Sarah's level. Furthermore, there were more important things to worry about, so it wasn't worth getting worked up over. like her quickly growing empire in business, for example.

Sarah pushed her chair back and marched off, leaving a bewildered bunch of former classmates in her wake. "Whatever," she muttered, "I'm going to go check out the school building, I'll be back soon, hopefully when there's a little less ego at the table."

"I apologize to all of you," Rivka stated. "I don't know why she is so worked up, I never did anything to her that would cause her to have that reaction"

Another woman remarked, "She's just really envious, and things aren't going too well for her personally. She sees you, the previous loser and geek, as everything she isn't, is divorced, and works in a soulless office job that doesn't showcase her people abilities."

"I should probably go talk to her, apologize for nothing I suppose," Rivka reflected. "I'd hate for her to have such anger in her heart for nothing"

Minky stopped Rivka as she got up to follow Sarah, asking,

"Where are you going? We had only just begun to enjoy ourselves!"

"It's crucial that I find Sarah and have a conversation with her," Rivka said.

"Well, return quickly! Already, you are missed!As Rivka turned to leave, Minky yelled.

Searching the school building's hallways, Rivka finally found Sarah, sipping from a drink as she stood close to the door of the 11th grade classroom. Taking a deep breath, Rivka moved toward Sarah, prepared to contain the situation, but as she got closer, she noticed the dress Sarah was wearing, a sleek black number that perfectly accentuated her curves, and she knew instantly that it was one of her own designs. Her mind raced as she tried to process the implications of this revelation.

"Tried to poke it in?Sarah spit out angrily.

"What in, rub?I really don't know what I have done to you,

Rivka shot back. In school, you treated me like trash, but I've moved past that. If I could, I would really like to know what is genuinely upsetting you. Please let me know."

"I'm sorry," Sarah muttered to Rivka as tears streamed down her cheeks. "I was wrong." I behaved completely inappropriately toward you both there and at school. I've felt bad about it ever since. However, seeing you here tonight, confident and successful, only made me remember all the horrible reasons I bullied you. To be honest, I kind of had a crush on you. Sarah's voice drifted off. "You were so pretty and smart, and I wasn't, and you had this quiet aura around you and..."

"Don't worry about it," Rivka said, drawing Sarah into a close embrace. "Let's put the past in the past, okay? Tonight, let's take it easy and enjoy the moment."

Sarah said, "I think I got some makeup on your dress, I'm sorry," with an embarrassed glance up at Rivka.

Rivka took in Sarah's features and added, "No worries, I have something in my car I can cover it with." "You really did this dress proud you know, it's almost as if it was designed for you"

"I know," Sarah replied, "I had to buy it the moment I saw it, your designs honestly make me feel confident and sexy, I'm sorry I mocked them before"

With a kind grin, Rivka said to her, "I've already forgiven you, so don't worry about it." Furthermore, thank you for the complement.

In response, Rivka wrapped her arms around Sarah's waist and pulled her closer as their tongues danced together, exploring each other's mouths in a passionate display of affection. Rivka began tracing the fabric with her fingertips, enjoying the way it made Sarah look. They stood there for a moment, staring into each other's eyes. Suddenly, Sarah leaned in close to Rivka, her lips inches from hers. Suddenly, she pressed them against her mouth, kissing her deeply.

After enjoying each other's company for a little while, they leaned forward and pressed lips to each other. Sarah hesitated at first, not sure if this was the right thing to do, but soon she found herself melting into the kiss as Rivka's tongue traced the outline of her lips. Their tongues danced together, tasting each other for the first time, and as they parted, they looked deeply into each other's eyes, feeling a connection that went beyond time and space.

Breathlessly, Rivka said, "Lock the door, and unzip that dress; I need to see you bare."

Without asking, Sarah obeyed, her hands shaking slightly as she unzipped the dress and let it fall to the floor, leaving no room for interpretation about the matching lace bra and panties set underneath, while Rivka's hungry eyes followed her every move, soaking in every inch of her body.

Reaching out to trace the exquisite lace of Sarah's underwear, she gasped, "So you're wearing my underwear as well? I really should have had you model them; you're breathtakingly beautiful."

Sarah leaned closer to Rivka, rubbing her body against hers and arching her back invitingly, blushing at the compliments, her cheeks turning red with excitement and humiliation.

Rivka dropped her head quickly and used her tongue and lips to feel every part of Sarah's body, from the tender skin of her neck to the fullness of her breasts.

She quickly and skillfully undid her bra's clasps with her hands.

Rivka's mouth watered as she took one nipple into her mouth and slowly suckled it while running her hand over the other breast. It slid to the ground, revealing gorgeous, round breasts that rose and fell with her hurried breathing.

With a loud sigh, head thrown back in sheer bliss, Sarah grasped at Rivka's hair, encouraging her on as she lost herself in the sensations racing through her body, urging her on as Rivka's gifted tongue flicked across her nipples.

Rivka wanted to enjoy every second of this meeting, to truly feel the wonderful pleasure of being with Sarah, but she was not in the mood to rush things.

So she slid down, kissing all the way down the valley between her breasts till she came to the hem of her panties, which she carefully pushed down, revealing a treasure trove of curls beneath, all while grinning mischievously.

Sarah bucked reflexively as the excruciating pressure developing inside her hips eased as Rivka's cool breath fanned across her heated flesh, sending waves of need rushing through her body and making her tremble.

Seeing the movement, Rivka grinned, understanding just

what Sarah needed to feel the exquisite folds of flesh buried inside her legs as she positioned herself between them and separated them wider.

Rivka gave in to the temptation and leaned forward to bury her face in the sweetness of Sarah's cunt, savoring the aroma of her excitement as she licked and suckled at her clit. Sarah's pussy was wet and eager for her, the folds of her labia shimmering with moisture.

With a shout of joy, Sarah flung back her head and felt Rivka's tongue playfully on her tender spot.

She bucked frantically, trying to get rid of the overwhelming pleasure that was flowing through her body by rubbing her hips on Rivka's face.

Rivka increased the intensity of her ministrations, tormenting and tease-ing Sarah's clit with her lips and teeth, knowing she had to keep up the pace, to keep Sarah on the verge of an orgasm without letting her tumble over the brink.

Sarah's orgasm swelled to a peak as Rivka's deft fingers teased and tickled her opening. She cried out again, her entire body trembling with pleasure as wave after wave of exquisite sensation swept over her.

At last, exhausted and content, she fell to the ground, and Rivka crept up next to her, putting her head on Sarah's shoulder while they both gasped for air.

Sarah said, "Thank you," as she was still gathering her thoughts.

"That was...amazing."

With a smile on her face and a silky, seductive voice, Rivka said, "Anytime," happy that she could make Sarah feel this way.

After lying there for a few more seconds, just enjoying each other's company, Sarah abruptly sat up with a playful glitter in her eye.

With a gesture toward Rivka's clothing, she continued, "Your turn."

Before Rivka could object, Sarah had taken off her shoes and was putting the finishing touches to her skirt, which gathered at her waist and exposed her nude body.

"Lie down on the floor," Sarah said, her eyes following the contour of Rivka's body and stopping at the round globes of her ass. With a nervous lick of her lips, Sarah wondered what was beneath those plump cheeks.

With little hesitation, Rivka lay flat on her back, gazing up at the ceiling as she felt Sarah's warm breath brush against her doorway and then began to push inside with one finger.

Sarah was gentle, easing another finger inside Rivka before adding a third, working them in and out of her tight channel, stretching her open and ready for more, until she was certain that Rivka was ready. When she was, she added a fourth finger, pushing deeper than ever before.

Rivka gasped at the sudden intrusion, her body tensing reflexively.

With a loud groan, Rivka's hips pushed forward to meet the onslaught; she was so satisfied, so completely filled by Sarah's touch, that any resistance went from her mind and she gave in to the pleasure that was pulsing through her body.

Once Sarah was satisfied that Rivka was ready, she took out her fingers and replaced them with her tongue, laving at the opening to her lover's pussy and taunting her with the promise of more pleasure to come. As Sarah continued to work her magic below, Rivka's hips thrashed wildly, her cries becoming more desperate and louder, and she clutched at her lover's hair, encouraging her to keep going as she lost herself in the sensations coursing through her body.

Unexpectedly, Sarah brought Rivka's legs up to her

shoulders and sank her tongue deep into her ass; Rivka cried out, shocked that she had never felt anything like this before; her hips bucking wildly, her ass clenching around Sarah's face as she rode out the intense pleasure; she could feel the heat building deep within her, the fire spreading throughout her entire body; she could feel the orgasm rising up within her, threatening to break free at any moment.

Sensing that an explosion was imminent, Sarah knew she had to move quickly. She slipped back between Rivka's legs and began to rub her clit rhythmically with one hand while fingering her ass with the other, feeling the tension in her body build to the brink of rupture.

Sarah held on tight, determined to see this through to the end, but then it happened: Rivka's muscles contracted fiercely, clamping down hard on her fingers as she rode out the intense pleasure. Her whole body convulsed, and her scream echoed off the walls as she was engulfed by a powerful orgasm.

Rivka's cries became more desperate as she wanted to get away from the amazing feelings that were flowing through her body, and she continued to stimulate her without stopping, not even for a moment.

At last, it abated, causing her to gasp for breath and tremble with subsequent shock waves.

Grinning at having been able to make her beloved happy in this way, Sarah kissed Rivka gently on the forehead before rolling off and sitting up.

Rivka uttered a soft "Wow," still collecting her breath.

She marveled at Sarah's elegant body lines as she extended her hand to trace the curvature of her spine. "You're amazing."

"You too," Sarah mumbled, reaching out to cup Rivka's breast as her cheeks turned crimson with shame and pleasure at the flattery.

"We need to stop this," Rivka laughed, arching her back into Sarah's touch. "People might see us if we continue." Rivka moaned.

Though her look was serious, Sarah nodded and said, "I don't want to lose contact with you," speaking slightly above a whisper.

"Neither do I," Rivka replied.

She took a time to think before speaking again. "What if I offered you a job?She made a hesitant suggestion.

Startled by the suggestion, Sarah arched her eyebrow. "Really? Like what?"

"As the manager of my flagship store," Rivka cheerfully disclosed, "I'm moving my current manager to one of the new stores to help them get on their feet." I was going to run an advertisement in the paper, but now that I think about it, you'd be ideal because of your people abilities. And I could see you all the time and..." she said, pausing thoughtfully.

Sarah smiled broadly after her eyes opened in shock "I'll take it!She excitedly cried out.

"Good," Rivka answered firmly, happy that Sarah had accepted her proposal. They looked into each other's eyes and felt their hearts beat in tandem.

With a slow, deliberate movement, Rivka came forward until her lips were only millimeters away from Sarah's, planting a scorching kiss on her lips.

Rivka's hands wandered freely over Sarah's body, tracing the curves of her hips and ass; Sarah responded in kind, running her fingers through Rivka's long hair and caressing her back as their tongues danced together, exploring the depths of one other's mouths.

Panting heavily, they broke apart to look into one other's eyes.

In return, Sarah encircled Rivka's waist with her arms,

drawing her closer as their bodies melted into one, their individual curves and contours perfectly fitting against one another.

Rivka withdrew first, breaking the kiss and laying her forehead on Sarah's, sighing contentedly. "We should go," she mumbled, but she made no attempt to walk away.

With a nod of understanding, Sarah said, "Okay," unwillingly releasing herself from Rivka's embrace as they walked back to the circle of friends, who gave them strange stares.

There were cheers and applause all around, and soon everyone was talking animatedly as Rivka rapidly filled them in on the details of the job offer and Sarah's acceptance.

Later in the evening, the talk turned to lighter fare, such as wedding preparations, childhood adventures, and travel destinations. Rivka found herself giggling and conversing with her old pals, relishing the companionship and reminiscences.

But her thoughts kept going back to Sarah, to the feel of her skin against hers, and the taste of her kisses; she couldn't help but wonder what would happen between them next.

Acknowledgments

The Glory of this book's success goes to God Almighty and my beautiful Family, Fans, Readers & well-wishers, Customers, and Friends for their endless support and encouragement.

About The Author

I've spent nearly a decade penning romantic novels. As a passionate writer of erotica, I craft dark, romantic erotica. Anime Naked Truth Se of Sacred Sexuality: Forbidden Seducing Short Stories of an Erotica Nude Sexy Girl Poster. Alongside Erotic Mystery Fiction, Victorian Erotica Sex, Black & African American Erotica, Euthanasia, Daddy Teaching, Forced Domination, Alpha Monster Cuckold, and BDSM for Adults, there's an Erotic Fiction in Kinky Family. I write dark, sensual romance because I adore the power of darkness and everything that it entails. Romance novels have always been my favorite kind of books, and now I'm writing them. The idea that you will like reading and enjoying my fiction as much as I enjoy pushing the frontiers of sexual pleasure in my writing thrills me more than anything else.